A CHANCE AT LOVE

DAKIARA

MIND FLOW PUBLISHING & PRODUCTION LLC

COPYRIGHT

First Printing: 2020

ISBN 978-1-951271-17-6 Paperback

ISBN 978-1-951271-16-9 Ebook

Additional copies of this book and others are available by mail or by visiting the website listed below. Check website for pricing.

Mind Flow Publishing & Production LLC

PO Box 48768 Cumberland, North Carolina 28331-8768

www.mindflowpublishingproduction.com

Cover Design by Carrie & Co.

Editing by Stories Matter Editing

Formatting Design by Clarity Townsend

Thank you for helping to bring A Chance at Love to life......

CHAPTER ONE

$\mathcal{H}$olly Mitchell has a lot going for herself. Most people her age would be a bit envious. From the latest Mercedes, to an amazing townhouse, that she owned free and clear thanks to some investments she had made when she was just 18 years of age. It was that moment, when she made the initial investment using her college savings on her 18th birthday she knew she wanted to be an investment broker. And now at the age of 28, she is a self-made millionaire, her choices have paid off. But Holly was not just any millionaire; she is beautiful to boot. To any man she would seem like a catch, brains, and beauty. There is one thing money cannot buy and that is love or happiness. Holly has always found it hard to know if someone really liked her for herself, or if there were ulterior motives. She has tried to date a few times, but the relationships never seemed to last long. Holly had all but given up on love, especially seeing the gaggle of women that her best friend runs through with no afterthought.

Benjamin Forrester knew he was the last on the short list

of male companions that Holly had. Ben was handsome and rich, but he had a problem, he was a compulsive liar. In the beginning he was so loving, so giving. All his time when he wasn't working was shared with Holly. Benjamin was her Prince Charming or so she thought. He would bring her flowers just because. From their first meeting when they both jumped into a taxi from opposite sides, and decided it was easier to share it. Holly had been interrogating him for information. "Why no girlfriend? Is there a Mrs. Forrester?" To which Benjamin replied, "Yes my mother." Holly didn't realize he had lied about being married until she saw a call coming in from someone named Samantha on his phone. The name was tagged with wife. Among his lies and his omissions, he left off the fact that he was bisexual. This information was given to her when Samantha reached out to her. She wanted to warn Holly of what she was getting in to. Holly didn't judge what others did, she always said that what went on between two consenting adults was fine by her, but she knew that wasn't the life for her. They parted ways after she told him she had an STD. He denied it of course, but then came clean a week later. Apparently, his wife Samantha also had it. Holly had never had a STD in her life and normally she would have been horrified, but given the high-risk lifestyle he was engaging in, it wasn't surprising. Benjamin was living the life of a "down low" man. Benjamin was hooking up with random guys and had been for years. Whenever he had business trips out of town, they weren't just business trips. He was going to the gay bars in whatever city he was in and picking up guys. He was living out his fantasy for couple of days, or a week at a time and then going back home to his wife and occasionally Holly. Holly was thankful that what she had wasn't something she would be battling with for the rest of her life. With Benjamin she had done the one thing she didn't normally do, and that was sleep with a man after only a few dates. *Never again*, she promised herself.

Holly had toyed around with the idea of trying to meet someone online, but the horror stories had her a bit leery and after the whole Benjamin ordeal, she was extra cautious. On a whim she decided to set up an online profile on a dating app called *"Meet Me"*. The company who built and operated the app, was owned by Brandon Thompson. Brandon and Holly had been best friends for the last 10 years since they met at Hinton University. They found out they shared a lot in common. Both were from single parent homes and from small towns. They were both the first one of their family to attend college. The two shared two classes one of which was English, which Holly hated. Brandon hated Economics, but of course Holly was amazing at it. During their sophomore year, they moved into the coed apartments together. It just seemed to make sense.

The two became inseparable and that is how things have stayed ever since. No matter who Brandon was dating at the time, he was always there when Holly reached out to him. There had been more than a time or two he had been accused of having a thing for Holly. Genesis, his latest fling of 6 months, even accused him of loving her.

"Of course, I love her. She has always been there for me. Why wouldn't I want to make sure she is always good? She's my best friend."

That didn't make Genesis feel any better about the current situation. Holly had called in the middle of their date night. Her SUV had run out of gas because she forgot, as she often did, to make sure there was plenty in the tank. Without hesitation, Brandon, told her he would be right there. Turning to Genesis, "Listen, I know you aren't going to like

3

this, but she is my friend. She needs me. I promised her years ago to always be there."

"Brandon, just go. You are going to do it anyway, no matter what I say about the matter. If you want to help her, why don't you get her a AAA membership."

Brandon knew she was right. There was no way he would leave Holly stranded, ever.

After the hour ride, Brandon pulled up to see Holly sitting on the hood of the vehicle. Only she could make sitting on a hood look like the thing to do. Brandon pulled up beside her and rolled the passenger side window down.

"Excuse me ma'am, but are those Bugle Boy jeans you're wearing?"

"I'm sorry. I didn't mean to interrupt your night. Was Genesis mad?" Holly opened the door to get in.

Holly already knew the answer to that question, but it was only right that she asked. Right?

Sighing deeply, Brandon told her of course Genesis was not thrilled, but she knew he was going to come. He always did.

She truly wanted Brandon to be happy with one girl versus all these short-term affairs that never lasted more than a year. Holly was surprised that he and Genesis was still trying to make it work. To be honest, Holly liked Genesis, but she knew she was just not for Brandon. She was gorgeous but still not the right fit for her friend. Brandon was more of a laid-back guy who just wanted to Netflix and chill. Genesis was always wanting to be out and about. She loved going to clubs and Brandon wasn't a big fan of that. He liked to live life a bit more reserved. Genesis had a thing about making sure she always ate out at the most exclusive and hottest or newest restaurants in town. Then there was the whole, she is an airhead and he is an Einstein, so their conversation was very limited at least as far as what Holly had witnessed to that point.

Snapping herself back to the present, Holly thought it would be a good time to throw out her request to Brandon again for help. Over the last few months, she had asked Brandon to introduce her to some of his friends. His answer without hesitation was always the same. *Nope not going to happen.*

"Bran, you do know that if you introduce me to some of your guy friends, you wouldn't always have to be the one I call. Besides, you can't keep all this hidden forever." Holly joked as she waved her hands on either side of her body, as if she were presenting a prize to be won on a game show.

As much as she annoyed Brandon with her theatrics he could only smile, and shake his head no.

"Who lied to you? You aren't no prize girl. More like a bothersome little sister."

Brandon told her that he had already called the tow truck and her car would be at her house before she woke in the morning. Stuff like this happened all the time. If it was not her running out of gas, she forgot or locked her keys in the car, had a few blown tires. Brandon had the towing company on speed dial. In most of the cases he could have just sent the tow truck, but Brandon always had to make sure she was good.

"Thanks again for coming for me. I am deeply sorry for being a burden."

Most of the mishaps that happened to Holly she could handle, but if she ever slipped up and it came out to Brandon and she didn't call him, he would flip out. That happened twice and that was more than enough for Holly to know, no matter what, always call Brandon. Holly had only witnessed Brandon pissed off a handful of times and three of them were over her. It was not something she cared to revisit unless it was unavoidable.

One of those times was during an Omega party on their rival's campus, Holly was attacked by a couple of guys. Holly was ready to go but Brandon wanted to hang out a bit longer with this girl Layla that he had just met. Holly knew it was bound to end up as a one-night stand so she told Brandon to stay and she would catch a cab back to campus. Brandon was wasted and not thinking clearly. Holly left the party and was standing outside looking up numbers for cab companies when she felt something hard hit her on the back of her head. The last thing she remembered was two guys talking nearby and then nothing but darkness. When she woke up, she was in the hospital with a concussion, a broken rib, and she had been raped. She didn't have any memory of the incident. That was the good news. From that day on Brandon was always there.

Brandon looked over at her, and he knew there was a few reasons why he wouldn't set her up with anyone. He didn't want to share her, plus his guy friends were flighty and they had little respect when it came to how they dealt with their women. Brandon didn't want to lose any business associates over Holly, but he knew it was a distinct possibility. To avoid it, he wouldn't connect her with any of them. He would rather deal with Holly giving him grief over it.

Holly asked him one more time during the ride home, about finding her a date with one of his friends. She knew deep down Brandon wasn't going to change his mind, but she felt she at least had to try.

Brandon dropped Holly off at home and told her he would see her tomorrow for lunch. He watched as she got out of the car and walked up the path to her townhouse. Once she was inside, she flickered the lights three times.

That had been their signal since forever. Driving off, Brandon tried to call Genesis. But there was no answer, not that he really expected one, so he left a voicemail.

"Hey Babe, I'm just getting back. I was just calling to see if you were still up. I guess not. Don't be mad about earlier, you know I had to go. If I didn't and something happened, I wouldn't be able to live with myself. Call me when you get this."

Holly felt restless when she got home. It was only then she realized that she had left her phone in the car. She used her house phone to call Brandon just so he wouldn't worry if she didn't answer her cell. She was slightly relieved that he did not answer this time, she hoped that meant that Genesis was on the phone with him. Holly decided to just leave a quick message for him.

"Hey, I know I just left you but wanted to make sure you knew that I was good, I left my phone in the car so I didn't want you to stress if I didn't answer. I would be lost without you my friend. Love you. Thank you again and goodnight."

Holly had barely hung up the phone before it rang. She answered knowing it had to be Brandon, not many had the number for her house.

"Hey, I just called you. I didn't want anything except to tell you thank you."

"No thanks needed. I will always be there. Even when you dance on my last nerve with those pointy shoes of yours."

They both laughed at that and said their goodnights.

After an hour or so of procrastination Holly decided to try and do a little homework on some new IPO's before finally calling it a night. Sitting Indian style on her bed with her laptop she was lost in her own world. After about an hour or so she took a small break from researching companies she was interested in to check her email. As she was skimming through them, she came across a message from someone named Trey on *"Meet Me"*. It was a basic message.

Hi, my name is Trey, I came across your profile and I would like to connect with you.

Curiosity got the better of her, and she clicked on the link attached. She needed to download the computer version of the app in order to view his profile and check any other messages she might have, which after a few clicks she did. After logging in she went to her messages and saw the same one from Trey, as well as one from someone named Joseph.

She clicked on Trey's profile and saw that he was thirty-two-year-old single man with no children and a business owner. Holly clicked through the pictures that were on his profile. This man was gorgeous. Chocolate with a low haircut, clean-cut and tall. That was a plus since Holly was 5'9 without heels.

She decided to message him back. She decided to get back to work and minimized the message. Holly took a bathroom break and by the time she returned, she had several messages from Trey.

"Hello, I'm glad you messaged me back. I was a little worried that I came on too strong in the preloaded message." (he sent several emoji smiley faces)

Smiling to herself, she wrote back.

"Yeah it was a bit overwhelming, but I couldn't resist the smile, and I could feel the sincerity in the message. LOL."

He immediately fired back.

"Wow, you spoke in a whole sentence. That is a definite plus young lady."

Holly admitted to herself, she was enjoying the conversation thus far as Trey's next message popped up.

"Ms. Holly, I must tell you, that you have me smiling over here. I know you may not believe it but I am. As much as I am enjoying

this, I do need to sign off. I have an early morning meeting I need to prepare for."

"I've got to sign off too. It has been nice chatting with you. Perhaps we can do this again soon."

"I would love it. There is also another option. You could join me for a lunch date on Saturday. Before you say no, just think about it. Today is only Sunday, I have plenty of time to hope."

She couldn't help but smile as she typed in her response.

"Fair enough, I will let you know. Good night to you."

"Night Night."

CHAPTER TWO

*H*olly woke up with a smile on her face the next morning, as the conversation with Trey crossed her thoughts. However, his time there was short lived. The phone on her bedside table let out a shrill ring and Holly knew it was Brandon. It was always Brandon, especially on the house phone. He wanted to remind her to get her phone from the car and to make sure they were still on for lunch.

As promised her SUV was waiting on her right outside. "Thanks, Bran, for all that you do. I'd be lost without you."

"Yeah, yeah, see you at lunch." She could hear the grin in his voice as he hung up the phone.

Holly had a 10 am hair appointment, and she could not be late. Even though she rocked out her natural curls, she still had to keep her hair healthy. Ebony, her stylist was amazing with her hands. She was the only one Holly trusted to touch her tresses. There was just one downside to it being her and Ebony in the shop alone. That girl stayed entrenched in her business. Her stylist always asked her was there anyone new in her life yet. "Or have you and Brandon decided to stop the charade?" Ebony has always shared that opinion, but she was wrong. Just like the others who always seemed to think they were an item.

"Actually, I'm working on that. And for the last time, Brandon is just my friend. My best friend to be exact."

"Oh yeah, please tell me more?"

Holly didn't have much to tell. She dared not to tell Ebony that she was considering going out on a date with a man she just met during a 5-minute chat session. All she had was some smiles left over from the short-lived conversation. Funny thing was she was still thinking about Trey and the conversation. *Dang that man was fine.* She thought as a smile crossed her face. Ebony had been her stylist for years now, and she knew of the debacle that happened with Benjamin. It took her sometime to get past it.

"I've started looking is all I'm going to say for now. I will let you know what happens, or if it works out."

"Un-huh. Make sure you do that Sis. Even a hard baller like yourself needs to be happy. You need someone to love. Plus, it may help you become less feisty. That's all I'm saying. By the way what's up with that gorgeous piece of delectable man candy Brandon? Tell him I'm still available."

Looking at her Michael Kors watch, Holly smiled to herself, it was almost lunch time. By the time Ebony had finished adding a protective sheen to her hair, Holly almost had to run out of there. She was pressed for time but also, she hated when Ebony sprayed her hair, the fumes would be everywhere. Thankfully the shop was only a block away from the restaurant that she and Brandon frequented and her hair had some time to air out.

Holly arrived at the Queen of Soul restaurant only to see that Brandon was already seated and waiting on her as usual. Every week for the last year and a half this was their place for lunch on Mondays. When she sat down, Holly was all smiles. Her thoughts kept drifting back to the conversation between she and Trey and the potential date. She thought about bringing it up to Brandon, especially since he wasn't trying to help her.

She sat there smiling after the waiter came and took their order.

"What is it? Why are you smiling like you know the secret to life?"

"You are nosy." Holly said with a cheeky smile.

"If you must know. Your girl got a date this Saturday. That is, if I say yes. And because you wouldn't find me a guy, I signed up for your site."

Brandon looked at her with disbelief. He had no knowledge of a new guy in his best friend's life. He could admit to himself that he didn't like the thought, but he would never talk about it to her. Brandon was getting slightly irritated.

"I think this guy could be the one. He kept me laughing. I truly smiled."

Brandon was shaking his head in disbelief as she was talking. Even after listening to her go on and on about how he just seemed right.

"Holly, you're too smart of a woman. How do you know he isn't running game on you? I know it's been awhile since you've had someone stable, but do you think this guy could be it from a 2-minute conversation?"

The waiter interrupted to set their plates down and refill their glasses.

Holly could not believe that he was acting this way. It's not as if she was going out with a stripper or something. She interacted through his site; didn't he trust his own vetting process?

They both sat in silence eating their food for a few

minutes. In their entire 10-year friendship, there hadn't been many disagreements between the two of them. When they bared down, they were stubborn just as their shared zodiac sign suggested. Those Taurus's although loyal, were stubborn as a bull, literally.

"So, you're going to really act like this is all normal. What if this guy is a killer? What if he is playing you? How can you possibly feel like he is the one from just a few minutes of exchanging messages, have you stopped to consider any of this? We have been friends for a long time, and I have never seen you this careless. Please tell me you didn't give him your home address or tell him anything about what you do?"

Holly rolled her eyes and sucked her teeth. Letting out a deep sigh as he was quizzing her. She couldn't believe he was being this way. Overprotective yes but was he serious right now.

"Bran, come on, please stop with the interrogation. I'm happy for once and I'm going to give this a shot. At least one date. You never know he could really be the one."

Brandon told her that she was a bit delusional and the app was just for fun and not to be searching for love. The two continued their debate back and forth. This made lunch a bit strained and tense. More than either would have liked it, but neither would budge on their opinion. The waiter only intervened in their discussion when it couldn't be helped. He quickly would move on after his business was finished, he dropped the check off early to prevent having to come back.

Becoming frustrated Brandon reached for the check, at the same time Holly did, but he was quicker.

"Give me that."

"Nah, I got it today. You save your money. You may have to treat Mr. Loverman."

"You are a complete jerk. It's one date for crying out loud. I never said anything about marrying the guy. Okay here, at least let me leave the tip."

"If that makes you feel better."

"If you were not my dearest friend, I'd be tempted to punch you. But I know you will punch me back and then we will both end up in jail. Resulting in no date for me. Besides Genesis would probably be a little miffed too."

This playful banter lightened the mood a smidge. After finishing up their meal, Holly noticed Brandon's face was still twisted up.

Holly stood up to leave, but not before kissing Brandon on the cheek. She always let her lips linger for a moment, that was something she hadn't paid attention to until that very moment. She noticed that he never pulled away from her either.

Turning to leave, she added, "Call me later. Please."

Brandon never responded. As she was walking away, she thought to herself. *He can't possibly be mad. Not seriously mad.*

Holly hadn't made it into the office yet today, and it was almost 2 pm. She called Cherise, her secretary, and told her to hold down the fort. That she wasn't going to be in this afternoon. She was a little frustrated with Brandon, but she was riding high from Trey's conversation and she refused to let him dampen her mood.

Holly decided instead of going straight home since it was so early, she would go shopping. It had been a few weeks since she had indulged in her favorite pastime. She found a perfect jumpsuit to wear for lunch with Trey. It was black and with a high neckline that was cutout at the front and back. Because she had health issues stemming from low iron and tended to be chilly, especially in restaurants, she got one with long sleeves. She was loving how it hugged her hips and thighs. Holly hoped he would like it.

Later that evening when she finally made it home, she called Brandon. He didn't answer, but instead sent her straight to voicemail. That almost never happened, but maybe he needed some time.

Once the tone sounded in her ear, she left him a message. "Hey Bran, I wanted to check on you and let you know I love you. I made it home, I know you'd be concerned if I didn't call and let you know. I know we didn't agree today but that happens. Talk to you soon."

CHAPTER THREE

Settling in to check her emails from the day, she saw there were a few messages in her inbox on the *"Meet Me"* App. There were a few from a guy named Alexander. She ignored the messages because for one, he didn't have a profile picture. He had a description, but no picture. That couldn't be a good sign. Secondly, he wasn't very descriptive either. He left a lot to the imagination. The only thing she could tell for sure was that he was a Dallas Cowboys football fan. The profile looked as if it was just started and he hadn't taken the time to finish it.

There was another message from Trey. She resisted responding right away. Maybe she was feeling things a little too much. She would slow things down a bit. Holly was still excited about the possibilities he presented though.

Trying to focus her mind back on her work emails and her computer chimed, signaling an incoming message. Holly notices that there is a new message from Alexander and within moments there is one from Trey. After finishing up reading and responding to her work emails she tried to call

Brandon again. Once again, he did not answer. This was so unlike him, but she was going to give him a little space. If he didn't answer tomorrow, she'd surprise him by bringing him lunch at work so they could talk things out.

Holly decided she would have a little fun before bed. She responded to Trey's message. He seemed genuinely glad to hear back from her.

"Hey Trey, how are you doing tonight? How was your day?"

Holly was so out of practice; she wasn't even sure she knew how to maintain a decent conversation with a man anymore. Who knows maybe he will get bored with her and the conversation and back out himself.

Trey didn't respond right away, this made Holly feel some type of way. To herself, Holly was thinking that Trey should have been eagerly waiting on her to message him back. Talk about an inflated ego. Instead of being patient she decided to message Alexander. After all what harm could it do?

"Good evening Alexander, I know it is late but, I wanted to just send out a quick hello. I also wanted to let you know that normally I wouldn't respond. Wait, before you get the wrong impression, not because I think I'm this or that, but because you don't have a profile picture. How do I know you are even real?"

"I assure you that I am real. And I get it. I also want to know someone is cool with just me, not the superficial. Thank you for responding back though. You stepped out of your comfort zone and took a chance, that says a lot about a person."

Holly wasn't prepared for Alexander's quick response. She thought it might scare him off. Yet it didn't. He still wanted to engage in a conversation. This intrigued Holly a little.

"By the way if there is something you would like to know, simply ask. I have no problem disclosing as long as you do the same."

Holly smiled and thought to herself that he was quite confident. She was digging it. It was refreshing.

They continued chatting back and forth. Alexander was a uproarious guy. He seemed to be down to earth and humble about where he came from and what he has done so far with his life. Alexander told her that he wasn't looking for love anymore, that when the right one came along, he would know it. He also shared that he was in a relationship. The relationship seemed to have been going off the rails for some time now.

Holly shook her head and thought, *another one of those.*

"Question, if you are involved, why are you on this dating site?" Holly had to poke the bear.

"Glad you asked. Told you, I'm not looking for love. The relationship she and I share has changed and not for the best. I'm not out here hunting if that is what you think. As you can see, I'm very upfront when it comes to that topic."

Holly couldn't deny that. She had to admit talking to Alexander wasn't full of pressure or anxiety. It was nice in fact. At that moment, her mind flashed back to Trey. He still hadn't messaged back. Maybe he was in bed already or working late. She decided not to stress over it.

Holly decided to send Brandon a text. Surprisingly, he responded but was very short with her. He said he was busy but would text back tomorrow. Holly thought to herself, *well at least he messaged me back. Hopefully he can't be still upset.*

Over the next few days Brandon and Holly played phone tag. She kept nagging him about what was going on and finally he told her. Genesis had cheated on him and he was trying to see if the relationship was worth saving. Holly didn't know how to help her friend. She never dealt with that particular issue before, if it was her, she would just cut ties. Her mindset was never stress about it. The right one will come along.

It was Wednesday night before Holly heard back from Trey. He popped back into her inbox like there hadn't just been radio silence for a few days. The more Holly looked at his profile, the more she began feeling him again. Was this simply a schoolgirl crush? Possibly so. All she knew was that the feeling kind of still felt good. Maybe it was just the thought of finding love that had butterflies fluttering in her stomach.

Holly agreed to go on the lunch date on Saturday with Trey. He said he was hoping that she would say yes. He shared that he knew she would. Even if it was nothing more than curiosity on her part. They said their good nights. Holly didn't even inquire about the silent treatment over the last few days. She was a little surprised that Trey didn't offer up any reason as to why it happened.

The rest of the week flew by in a blur. Holly's anxiety began to flare as the date got closer and closer. She began to question if it was the right thing to do or if she was moving too fast.

The one thing that was calming her nerves was the consistent messages from Alexander. He seemed to always know when she needed an ear to listen. Holly found herself venting to him about Brandon and like a good friend he simply listened. Her conversation with Brandon was very light these days. When they did chat, it was via text message, and about nothing serious. Just quick check-ins. Holly felt like they were drifting apart. She did miss him and his friendship of course. Alexander assured her that all would be okay. He suggested that Brandon probably just needed time to work through his own drama and didn't want to include her in that.

Finally, Saturday arrived, and Holly was a ball of nerves. She and Trey had agreed to meet at Vin Rouge, a French restaurant at 1 pm. When she arrived, Trey was already there waiting for her. She instinctively looked at her watch, she was 10 minutes early. She was proud of herself. His picture didn't do him true justice. Trey was tall and slim, but not too thin. His skin was a rich cocoa brown. She noticed his eyes were hazel. Holly had to catch herself and stop staring. She was trying to determine if they were his eyes or if he was wearing some of those contacts that change one's eye color. They were his, she eventually determined.

Trey eyed her up and down as well. He liked what he saw. She was gorgeous but didn't seem overly sure of herself like some women he was used to. Trey greeted her with a hug and a quick peck on the cheek. As the hostess escorted them to their awaiting booth, Holly noticed that Trey guided her in the direction of the booth. This was different. She also noticed that they were walking on rose petals and there were two roses on their table. Turning to Trey, she asked if he was responsible for that, he only smiled, and took her coat before she slid into the booth.

Surprisingly enough Holly was enjoying Trey's company. They ordered some drinks to start and a few appetizers. Holly could feel a little strain in trying to make sure she said the right things and wasn't too overbearing, or acted as if she was helpless like she did with Brandon sometimes. Holly made sure she only had two drinks, although Trey had four. He seemed to handle his alcohol well. If Holly would have taken the chance on more than two drinks, she wouldn't be able to stand. Her tolerance was so low it was almost nonexistent.

The waiter had just delivered their main course when Holly's phone went off. She didn't answer it, she knew it had to be Brandon because of the specific ringtone that she had assigned him. The phone continued to ring, and she continued to ignore it. Trey on the other hand didn't.

"Are you going to get that?" Trey seemed annoyed.

Holly couldn't blame him. Brandon knew she was out on her date. The only reason he should have called was if there was an emergency. Holly knew in her gut that wasn't the case though.

"No, I'm not. It is my best friend. He can wait until I get home tonight."

Holly tried to sound reassuring that she was focused on the date at hand. Trying to move past it, she began asking Trey questions about his family. The distraction didn't work. Mid question the phone went off again, this time she quickly hit the reject button. Why hadn't she simply done that in the beginning? Could have saved a lot of drama.

The food looked good and they began to eat.

"Pardon me folks. I was told by my manager, and the owner to ask you both to leave immediately. Apparently, there was a complaint of some sort. He doesn't want any trouble."

Trey could see the embarrassment painted across Holly's face and the fury flare to life in her eyes. He didn't know what was going on between her and her best friend but whatever it was it wasn't going to be pretty when it finally came to a head.

Standing up and walking around to Holly's chair without speaking he slid her chair back and offered her a hand to help her stand up.

"You are making a big mistake, but we will leave. The food wasn't that great anyway." Holly was a little surprised by Trey's outburst. He reached into his wallet and threw some cash on the table. Trey left more than enough to cover the meal; he was proving a point. As they were walking toward the front of the restaurant Trey turned looking over his shoulders to glare at the waiter.

When they reached the door that led to outside, Holly tried to offer up an apology. She could tell Trey was bothered by it but he gallantly tried to make her feel better. Holly told him that she would talk to him soon. As she turned to walk away, she pulls her phone out and begins calling Brandon's phone. But of course, like the jerk he was being, he didn't answer the phone. This infuriated Holly even more. She left him a series of voicemails each one more hostile than the previous.

CHAPTER FOUR

*A*fter Holly made it home safely and had calmed down, she decided to call Trey. They had exchanged numbers at the restaurant. Without prompting he had brought up the time when there was no conversation for a few days. He was dealing with an ex and she didn't want to move on. She had smashed his computer and his phone when they had gotten into a heated argument. He couldn't believe that she went so far as to throw his stuff out of the twenty-story high-rise window. Luckily, she didn't hit anyone with it. It took a few days for him to replace his items. Holly enjoyed his company, so she accepted his answer to a question she desperately wanted answered.

Holly apologized to him about the way the date ended. Trey was bothered earlier but now over the phone he was a being a good sport about it. He said he could see why any man would act a fool over her. Even if they were only friends. She was amazing, and he really enjoyed their time together, so he told her time and time again. Holly blushed.

Trey asked if they could have a do over. Holly readily

agreed and the two of them decided to do it the next day. They continued talking for over an hour. Neither of them it seemed wanted to get off the phone, but they both had other obligations.

Holly decided to try Brandon again. This time he answered. She ripped into him with the fury of a woman scorned. Brandon tried to interrupt her several times but to no avail. He decided to allow her to get it out of her system first. If she only realized that he only wanted what was best for her. Holly was in no mood to listen. Her rant continued for a full 10 minutes. Brandon had to admit he had only seen her this upset a few times. Without warning, she finishes her verbal assault on him and hangs up.

Brandon thought it was a mistake but when he tried to call her back. No answer. He called again, and her phone went straight to voicemail. Now it was his turn to leave her a few messages. Brandon tried to choose his words very carefully because he knew that his friend would twist them when she was this upset. He also sent a few texts throughout the rest of the night.

I just wanted to say that I had a good time. Don't worry about it, everything will work out, I can't wait to see you again tomorrow.

Trey's message came across as she laid across her bed. She thought that he was thoughtful. But she refrained from responding back.

Her computer sounded off again. She thought it was Trey again, but it wasn't. It was Alexander.

A smile crept to her face. She was pleasantly surprised. He was asking how she was. Did she do anything exciting. She tried to dissuade him by telling him that her day was horrible. She thought he was going to cut the conversation short, but instead he tried to pull more out of her. This was a welcoming feeling especially considering the day she had.

The more he asked, the more she disclosed. They went back and forth for hours. Alexander was understanding and on her side. He tried to reassure her that her best friend had the best of intentions, but Holly wasn't trying to hear it.

She began to feel more at ease, and she liked the fact that she could be herself with him. Holly didn't have to pretend or act a certain way. Just herself. Alexander remained consistent so far. He had her feeling better and even giggling a little before too long. Before she knew it, she had drifted off to sleep messaging him.

Holly woke up around 3:30 in the morning with her laptop beside her and the messenger app open. She had fallen asleep in the middle of replying to his message. Alexander had messaged her several times since her message. He was trying to make sure everything was okay. After a few tries he signed off. Holly left him a quick message to explain what happened. She then turned her laptop off and drifted blissfully back to sleep.

CHAPTER FIVE

*H*olly rolled over and grabbed her laptop to see if Alexander had received her messages. So far there was no reply. What could she honestly expect, she did fall asleep on him mid conversation. Holly was a little disappointed. She decided she would get herself up and go for a much-needed run. It had been a few weeks since she did that. That was her outlet when she needed to clear her head. Holly left and went up the block, past the high school and through the park and came back the same way. Her standard run was about 5 miles unless she was mad or with something weighing on her mind. Today was just for fun and needing to get back into her routine run. When the mad runs came about, she would run for close to 10 miles. When she returned home, she checked her email and then went to take her shower.

The water felt good against her skin. These last few days had taken its toll. Today she was able to enjoy her shower without rushing. She and Trey did have a date, but it wasn't until later that day. Holly was kind of geeked up about it. But, for now she was going to enjoy her peaceful time.

After her shower she was getting dressed and going through her closet to pick out her outfit for her lunch date. She narrowed her choice down to two, one was a dark denim jean set and the other was a lime green linen pantsuit. When she wore the lime green pantsuit, she always received glowing compliments. She hoped Trey liked it too. At that thought, she made her mind up about the pantsuit.

"Yep, that's the one."

As she was hanging the clothes back up into the closet, her phone started ringing. She answered without looking at the caller ID. She was pleasantly surprised it was Trey.

"Hey Holly. How are you doing this morning?"

"I'm okay. Funny of you to call. I was just thinking about you. Well more like about the outfit that I'm wearing for our date later. I think you will like it."

Holly was smiling as she talked.

"I hate to do this, but I need to cancel... well more like reschedule."

He was not prepared for the silence that met his statement. Holly drew in a deep breath and gathered her thoughts.

"I am a little disappointed. But I do understand. Things happen. Are we going to reschedule or just wait to see what happens?"

She tried to sound optimistic but couldn't help thinking that he was pulling back due to Brandon and his shenanigans. Holly really hoped that it wasn't the case. Maybe something had honestly come up. All she could do was just be patient.

They talked some more. Trey tried to assure her things were good. The two of them laughed and joked a little about the restaurant. Both had thick skin, so it didn't bother them too much that other people were watching. Thankfully, the waiter spoke to them in hushed tones.

Trey mentions that he must go and that he would call her soon and they would make plans to meet up. She agreed and they hang up. Holly's mind kept going back to him cancelling the date.

Suddenly the sound of someone knocking on her door drifted into her bedroom.

"Who is it?"

She hurried through the foyer to make it to the front door, afraid that something was wrong, given the urgency of whoever was on the other side of her door.

"Really, one or the other?"

Holly yelled as she opened the door, only to see Brandon there. She immediately became more annoyed. She knew it had to be someone being silly but still. Why do it?

Brandon was all smiles and holding something behind his back.

"Don't be mad. I really thought you weren't going to open the door. But I have something for you."

Brandon pulled his left hand from behind his back slowly. He had the beautiful bouquet of red and pink roses, with a yellow and a white one included. Holly smiled a little, but her smile got bigger when he brought his right hand from behind his back. Brandon had brought her breakfast from IHOP, one of her favorite breakfast places.

Grabbing the flowers and turning to head back into the house careful not to let the door close, so Brandon knew it was safe to enter.

"Thank you but, you know this still doesn't make it right?"

"Yeah, I know, but hopefully it is a start. I truly apologize.

I'm not sure why I did what I did. I know it was out of love. I just don't want to see someone mess over you or treat you wrong. I'm always used to you being here when I need you. I guess I spazzed. That won't happen again."

Brandon spoke sincerely and he only hoped that she could find it in her heart to forgive him.

Holly walked a little closer to him to close the gap and reached out her hand to him. Placing a hand on either side of his face, she turned his face towards her. She placed a kiss on each of his eyelids. Holly always loved his eyes; they were mesmerizing and always drew her in making her mind wander to places it shouldn't. They were just friends, always have been, always will be.

"Bran, you are my oldest and dearest friend. My best friend. You have always had my back and I forever will have yours. No matter what or who comes into our lives. Yes, before you say it, I know you have sacrificed so much of yourself when it comes to relationships because of me. I am forever grateful. I'm also sorry that I have been a burden in that way to you. I see it now clear as day. Because you have danced all over my last few nerves."

She said the last part with a smile on her face. Brandon had pulled away from her to arm's length. He couldn't think straight when she did that eyelid kissing thing. If she only knew what it did to him and his senses, she would probably think twice about it. Refocusing his thoughts, he began again.

"Holly, you have to trust me, it was all in your best interest. I would never do anything to purposely hurt you. Please trust me."

"I do."

That answer given in all its simplicity sent a shiver

through Brandon's spine. He shook it off. He was happy that she was willing to forgive him and trust him again.

Brandon mentioned that there is a new movie that just came out two days ago that he was wanting to see. If she was up to it, they could hit up their favorite movie theatre. After they ate breakfast of course. They decided on the matinee showing so they could get ready for their week ahead. They were both fans of the Marvel Universe films and were both waiting to see it with the other.

While eating breakfast they talked, they laughed, and all was forgiven.

They laughed and talked like they hadn't in the last few weeks or so.

While at the theater they were laughing so hard and talking. Brandon just knew someone was going to say something about their talking through the movie. He was surprised when no one did. The movie lasted 3 hours and afterwards they went to a Thai restaurant. Holly knew it was Brandon's favorite. It was kind of funny because for someone who didn't like spicy food, he would indulge in it only to suffer the consequences later.

When they got back in the vehicle after dinner, Holly was the first to speak.

"Thank you for today Brandon. I really enjoyed it. Reminded me of the old days."

Brandon agreed. Today was stress free and that was how life should be. He didn't want the day to end or for him to somehow ruin it. He kissed her on the cheek after walking her to the door, when they arrived at her house. Surprised she asked if he was coming in. Brandon declined and said he had a couple of business meetings to get ready for.

"Thank you for accepting my apology and being my friend. You know I love you right?"

Holly smiled before turning to unlock the door. Once inside and the door was closed, she whispered, "I love you too."

Even she had to admit, today was pretty good. She had somehow forgotten that Trey had cancelled on her. And with being honest with herself, she hadn't thought about him at all the whole day since they spoke earlier. There was one person who kept entering her thoughts from time to time, and that person was Alexander.

To help clear her mind and get ready for bed, she decided to take a shower. While in the shower she allowed herself to imagine what Alexander might look like. Holly thought he would have a fair complexion with broad shoulders, hazel eyes, and a bald fade. He incontestably wore an earring in his ear. She always found that to be sexy.

Feeling refreshed from her shower she decided to quickly check her email to make sure no one from work had any issues that she needed to get in front of before work tomorrow. Holly checked her app and there were no messages from either guy. She reached out to them just to say hi and good night. Holly closed the lid of her computer and turned over and within minutes she was out like a light.

CHAPTER SIX

$\mathcal{T}$he next morning Holly woke up feeling well rested. That was a great thing because she had a early meeting and then it was off to lunch with Brandon. She reached for her phone so she could text him to make sure they were still on for their lunch date. Brandon told her he would have to let her know, as it got closer to lunchtime. He had a few meetings, was hoping they wouldn't run over. Holly understood and told him they could just push it back to next week if they needed to. That way no one felt rushed. It was a good thing that she cancelled the lunch date because her own meeting went longer making her late for her hair appointment.

While under the dryer at the salon she gets a notification from the "*Meet Me*" app. It was from Alexander. She immediately smiled. Ebony didn't miss a beat. She had been trying to get information out of Holly since she arrived. Holly wasn't giving it up. When she caught her smiling, she started picking on her and saying "Ohhhhhh you in love huh?"

Holly just side eyed her and continued to check her

messages. There was one from Trey as well. She responded to Alexander's first.

"Thank you for checking in on me. My day is going well. A lot of meetings and I've been running late all day. But that's enough about me. What's going on in your world?"

"That sounds very busy. I don't mean to disturb you and your day. Just wanted you to know you were being thought about."

Holly caught him up on what had been going on with Brandon and Trey. She told him that she was a little disheartened with Trey cancelling on her, but she was taking it in stride. Alexander never made her feel awkward or like a brat for sharing and just conversing.

Alexander and Holly chatted more frequently over the next few days. He always seemed accessible when she needed to vent about her day, or just talk in general. He was a breath of fresh air.

Wednesday evening Trey texted Holly and asked if she was free this upcoming weekend. Holly hesitated on responding. She wanted to see if he would sweat a little. Trey texted again, and then he called.

"Hey Holly, listen I know you are probably busy but just think about it and let me know if you are free this weekend. If not, it's okay we can do it another time." Trey jumped right into the conversation without letting her say hello first. He was feeling a bit nervous apparently.

"I was just about to text you. I just got out of the shower."

Holly fibbed to see if she could get a response from Trey. She was trying to gauge where his head was at. He let out a deep breath. Holly smiled to herself.

"It looks as if I'm free this Saturday for most of the day. What did you have in mind?"

"I thought to make up for the last date, we could go to the

park and have a picnic. Maybe we won't be interrupted. Whatcha think?"

"Sounds great. Looking forward to it. We'll talk soon. I've got to go."

Holly wanted to be the first one to hang up. She was a little petty like that. It always seemed as if he was dipping out on her.

"I just wanted to check in on you. We hadn't spoken today," came the message from Alexander.

Holly smiled; she was getting used to his messages. He never forced the issue of getting her number or meeting face to face. Alexander was just easy. Holly filled him in on her plans for the weekend. He told her he had a date himself. Holly was a little taken back by that for some reason she didn't expect him to say that or perhaps she just didn't want to hear it.

"That is great. Good to hear you are getting out. I want you to tell me all about this mystery lady. Starting now."

"Well this may sound crazy, but I feel such a connection with her. She reminds me of you a little. Don't get weirded out. I just mean that she is easy to talk to and there is no pressure. She is in between relationships. We are kind of on the same path right now. Both just getting out there and testing the waters a bit."

The two continued chatting for a bit, before Holly said that she needed to get to bed.

Right before she was about to lay down, Brandon texted Holly.

"I just wanted to say good night to my best friend. I know things were weird with us for a bit, but I feel they are much better now. Just know that I love you and I will always be here for you."

Holly smiled as she texted back a quick reply, *"Yeah me too. Always."*

Holly and Brandon were finally back to normal. He was

his usual self. Brandon even joked around about maybe Holly will finally get some action and be her kind self again. Holly noticed that the closer that it got to Saturday, Brandon became scarce. He told he that he was thinking about possibly starting to use the app himself especially if she can find love on it.

Brandon told her to have fun on her date and that he wanted to hear all about it afterwards.

"You really want to hear about my date?"

"Of course, anything that makes you happy, makes me happy. Come on man, how long have we been best friends?"

Throughout the week Alexander makes sure that he stays in contact with her. He would even reassure her that she was right to explore all options. She deserved to be happy after all.

The closer that it got to the weekend, the more excited Holly became. She purchased this cute romper that was turquoise and black from Macy's earlier that week, thinking it would be perfect for a relaxing day spent in the park. Holly texted Trey to make sure that they were on still for the picnic and he told her yes of course, he couldn't wait.

Holly wasn't leery anymore about Brandon popping out from behind the bushes on them. She was so confident that she told him exactly where they would be. This was just a test to make sure he was okay she really didn't believe him. But he deserved the benefit of the doubt. She couldn't imagine losing her best friend or having to choose between a boo thang or her best friend.

Friday night it was Alexander who messaged her until she fell asleep. She hadn't heard a word from Trey other than when she messaged him to make sure they were still on. They agreed to meet at the park. Holly said she would make the food, all he had to do was show up.

CHAPTER SEVEN

*B*right and early Saturday morning, Trey messaged Holly the time they were supposed to meet up. She didn't get it until she was finished showering and eating breakfast. While watching TV and eating she began scrolling through her messages. Holly felt a flutter in her tummy. She liked Trey well enough, she just hoped he was the real deal. When they began communicating, she realized now that she did jump into it headfirst. So maybe Brandon had a reason for getting weird on her. She smiled as she continued to check her messages and her emails. There was no surprise that there were a few from Alexander. He hadn't missed too many days without sending her a good morning message and a good night one. Thinking back on it now, she kind of kept her eyes peeled for them. When her day was rough or just long it was good to have a person who she could unwind with. For a long time that person was Brandon, but the reality was that he couldn't always be there for her. She must allow him to lead his own life.

Realizing that she still had a lot of time before the picnic, she decided to lay back down for a while. That didn't last long. Alexander was in her inbox.

"Hey there Sunshine. I hope things are good for you today."

He was so sweet and thoughtful. Holly had confided in him about the picnic. She also told him that she was having some anxiety about it. She thought Trey was cool and all, but what if Brandon acting out was a sign. The whole time Alexander kept reassuring her that it would all work out. Your best friend is only protecting you from the unknown, he told her.

"Hey yourself. So far so good. You know I have that thing today."

"You mean your little picnic? That's right, that is today huh? It will be fine. Hopefully you can enjoy yourself. Oh, wait where is your best friend? Lol." She chuckled as she read the message.

"Oh, you want to be funny. You came with the jokes today huh? Cute. He is busy with work and I think he is dating someone. It seems like everyone in my world is doing that these days, including you."

"We can't let you have all the fun. Can we?"

"Yeah I guess not. I was just about to lay down for a bit and ask you if I could message you later? If you weren't too busy with your mystery woman, but you can't leave me hanging like that."

Holly said it jokingly, but she was kind of curious about this lady who had captured his attention. She didn't want to pry just yet. Knowing she did not have time to devote to taking a nap, she was starting to feel anxious butterflies take hold in her belly in anticipation of the picnic, but she was also enjoying the conversation.

After messaging for another hour or so, Holly finally said she needed to go and start getting ready.

"You will be fine. Enjoy yourself and we will compare notes later." was the last message she received from Alexander.

Holly arrived a little early to the meeting spot. She was anxious to get things set up. Holly also didn't want him having to sit and wait for her. As she was finishing up laying everything out, she looks up and sees Trey walking towards her. He is dressed in some linen slacks, a polo top, and some sandals. As he got closer, she couldn't help but look down to his feet. *Nice*, she thought. His feet were sporting a freshly done pedicure. Holly smiled; Trey also smiled because he knew she checked his feet out. He reached out to give her an embrace and a kiss on the cheek, handing her the single rose he was carrying.

"Oh, I saw you woman. You are checking me out. Do I pass inspection?" Trey teased her.

"Absolutely and then some. Glad to see you could make it. Now where did you find this beautiful purple rose?"

"Me too. Umm, none of your business, a man's gotta keep his florist secrets close to the vest. Now let's get to it." he said rubbing his hands together and grinning.

Trey helped her down to the ground, and then sat himself. The two shared some pleasant conversation over fruits, wine, and sandwiches. They talked about work, about their upbringing. They both agreed this was the real first date.

"This was a great suggestion. It's been awhile since I had been on a picnic, and today was a great day for it."

"Thank you for giving this another chance. I know you are a little torn because of your best friend and it is rightfully so. I do not want you to feel any pressure, but I do enjoy your company. I am glad you clicked on my message on *"Meet Me"*.

All Holly could do at the time was smile. She was feeling

relaxed. It could have been the wine, but she wanted to believe Trey had something to do with it as well.

After sitting, talking and people watching, the pair decided to take a walk through the park. Trey began packing things up neatly and placing into the basket that Holly had brought with her. It wasn't until then that he thought about the fact, he invited her to a picnic, yet she took over the idea about a day later. Smiling to himself he thought she did a great job with it. Once he finished, Trey reached down to assist her up.

"My mom always told me if the woman cooks the man cleans."

"It seems your mom raised you correctly. I wish more men understood that concept. The world would be so much better. It is refreshing to see that though, seriously."

The pair walked hand in hand towards the man-made lake on the northside of the park. There was some bread left so they were able to feed the ducks that joined them on the bridge. They talked some more as they saw a few fish come up for air and some crumbs.

Trey's eyes stayed on Holly as the wind blew through her hair, and the sun kissed her cheeks. Her profile picture didn't do her true justice. She was stunning. She knew it too. Her confidence was mesmerizing.

Holly tugged on his hand to snap him out of his daze.

"Hey where did you go? I thought I lost you for a minute there."

"I was just thinking. Thinking about you and how lucky I am to know you right now. I wish today could last for a long time."

Trey brought Holly's hand up to place a kiss on it. He then laid her palm against his cheek. Holly thought to herself, *today seems almost perfect.*

They continued their walk until they made it back to the parking lot. Trey put the basket in the backseat and opened her driver's side door. Holly leaned in to kiss him, he wrapped his arms around her, pulling her close. The kiss itself was underwhelming. It lacked that special something.

She smiled and told him she would call him later as she got into her car.

During the drive home, Holly's mind was all over the place. How could a perfect day leave her so unfulfilled? Trey was suave, and charming. He was handsome and was also financially secure. Holly misjudged the book. She assumed that Trey was going to be firing on all cylinders. Holly spent too much time dreaming about this guy and he didn't measure up. In her thoughts his kisses would send electric currents through her entire soul. If anything, the flame was smoldering at best. That would never be enough for her or could it? She chastised herself the rest of the drive home because it was her fault for hyping him up. A thought crossed her mind, she almost wished Brandon would have crashed the date. At least that way she wouldn't know this feeling, at least not yet. She laughed to herself at the thought of Brandon. *He is going to get a kick out of this.*

Holly made a few stops on her way home. She desperately needed some butter pecan ice cream to help clear her mind so she could figure this all out.

Once she arrived home, she showered, changed, and pulled out one of her favorite books of poetry by DaKiara entitled *Spoken from the Heart*. Other than her going running, reading was another way to relax her mind.

Holly decided to make herself some hot tea as well. While the water was boiling, she thought about Alexander. They were supposed to compare notes about their outings. Walking back into her bedroom she grabbed her laptop and decided to message him. She typed up a quick message to say she was checking in. Holly went back to making her tea and getting settled on the bed with her book and laptop.

Just as she was picking up her book to begin reading, she heard that all too familiar chime from the computer letting her know that Alexander was waiting. She smiled and checked his message.

"Hey there."

"Hey yourself. How was your date?" Alexander replied

"Well my bestie didn't crash the date this time. So that part was great. Are you sure you want to talk about this?"

"Of course, we are friends, right? Friends talk about everything. Let's hear it."

"If you insist. But don't say I didn't warn you. Trey is amazing. In most departments. He has his own financial security, gorgeous to look at, he is smart, kind, and he made me feel like I was the most important woman in the world today. Yet, at the end when we kissed. There was nothing. No spark. No friction. Just nothing. Maybe I'm expecting too much. What do you think? Should I be chill and enjoy the time?"

"Baby girl, everyone wants to feel sparks. We all deserve it. If the sparks aren't there, don't force it."

"I just don't want to be an a-hole and miss out on something great because maybe today was just a bad day for him in that department." Holly sighed deeply as she hit send on the message.

They talked some more, and Alexander tried to be supportive. He told her, the right one would be there for her. He advised her to just take her time and enjoy life.

"Maybe you should check with Brandon and see what he thinks? Maybe he can advise you on what to do, without sounding selfish."

"*Maybe I will but I don't want to hear any of his I told you so crap.*"

Holly and Alexander laughed equally as hard. The more she chatted with Alexander the easier it felt and the more comfortable she was. Before she knew it, they had been talking for almost 2 hours.

"*I'm going to go read this book and eat my ice cream so I can get my mind right. If you're not busy maybe I will message you later.*"

Alexander was hesitant on responding right away. His mind was on whether he should ask her a question. One simple question. He decided to go for it. If she shot it down, well, at least he asked.

"*Hey Holly, I was thinking if you would like to hang out sometime. No pressure or anything. We don't have to call it a date.*"

Holly was a little shocked by the question. She enjoyed the conversation but for gosh sakes she had never seen a picture of him. What if he was the real psycho Brandon was concerned about?

Almost as if sensing her reluctance, Alexander messaged back.

"*It's okay. Forget that I asked. I don't want you to be uncomfortable.*"

"*It's not that persay. I just thought we were cool but, yeah we can make a date.*"

"*Whew, you had me worried for a moment there. Thank you for saying yes. I promise you won't regret it. Would Friday be okay?*"

Holly agreed to Friday and they picked a place. It was one that Holly had wanted to try for some time, Madame Croix. The two decided 7:30pm sharp would be the time that worked best for them both.

Holly thought she would feel anxious about the date, but

she didn't. She didn't expect it, but she was okay with it. *OMG what is Brandon going to say?*

They ended their conversation and Holly retrieved her ice cream from the kitchen and snuggled in to read her book. Before she drifted off to sleep after making it halfway through the poetry book, her last thoughts were of Brandon.

CHAPTER EIGHT

$\mathcal{T}$he next morning Holly woke up and decided to head out for a run. She was trying to gradually get herself back into a routine. While running she thought more about Alexander and his invitation for a date on Friday. The more she thought about it, the more she decided that she would reach out to her best friend, he would know what she should do. Even if she didn't really want to hear it.

After her run and shower she gave Brandon a call, he answers on the third ring.

"What's up Holly?"

"Hey Bran Bran. I was just hoping to talk to you. It's been a few days."

"We've gone longer without talking before. Don't you remember? I take it your date thingy went okay?"

"Hey, what's going on with you? Are you okay? You seem, I don't know, different. Or am I bothering you right now?"

"It's nothing like that. Work has had me all over the place. I've always got time for you. Well most of the time."

Holly goes into her sob story about what happened on

her date. She felt that Brandon was only half listening to her. To test her theory, she throws in the mix of her conversation that she is pregnant. She couldn't believe it. Not a peep did he make. It wasn't like him to be this distracted.

"Brandon! What gives man? I'm trying to ask you for advice and you're not listening."

Brandon let out a deep sigh before he proceeded with the conversation. She knew he was rubbing his head. He often did that when he was frustrated.

"Holly, listen, I told you to not go out with the guy. Perhaps I was wrong. You had a good time and that is what matters. The other stuff will come."

That was it. That was all he had to say.

"I hate to rush you off the phone Holly, but I've got to get ready for my date."

Holly almost choked on the air caught in her throat. *Wait, did he just say date? Who is this woman? Where did she come from and why hadn't my best friend shared this before? Usually before he would take someone out, he would have shared details. Where they met, where was she from? Her credit score, and what her parents did. But nothing with this woman. That was highly unusual.* She sighed deeper than she would have liked.

"Holly I'm grown, you're grown. I can date. Best friend rules state as much."

Brandon was being a jerk, but Holly got it. She had to ease back and give him some space. He gave her some, even though he didn't particularly agree.

"Alright, well I'm going to let you go and do your thing. Call me later if it's not too late. Make sure you let me know you made it home okay. Love you."

"Love you too."

This was one of the few times Holly felt pushed to the side, but she knew Brandon is entitled to a life. Didn't mean she had to like it. Holly felt it doubly when she messaged Alexander and he didn't respond. She felt kind of a like a jerk for sitting there and actually waiting for him to.

Holly needed to talk and just wanted to feel like she wasn't alone. She went and got her butter pecan ice cream from the freezer, that always made her feel better until it didn't. Her mind was still going a thousand miles a minute. She thought about just taking a long hot and relaxing shower to melt away the foolery of the day but changed her mind and decided on a run to work off the ice cream she just inhaled. Holly couldn't believe she had eaten half of a carton. She needed to clear her mind and escape.

Before putting on her running gear she texted Brandon and told him she was going out for a run. Better to be safe than sorry. By the time she finished dressing he had messaged back a simple *"Be safe",* then within a moment another message, *"Let me know when you are back home."*

"Blahhhh."

Holly still hadn't heard anything from Alexander either. This wasn't the first time so she shouldn't have been in an uproar.

These men have lives. Just because you got comfortable with having access doesn't mean you are the only one with access.

Grabbing her keys, she headed out, making sure to lock the door behind her. One night she had gone for a run and when she returned the whole door was wide open. Holly had never been so terrified in her life. But who did she call, and who came running to make sure nothing was missing, and no one was inside? Good old Brandon. He warned her about going out running after dark, but she said she needed it sometimes. He had often gone with her to make sure she was okay. Holly truly never thought about these things. The very things she took for granted. She just assumed he would always be around. She made a mental note to tell him that she appreciates him more.

With no clear destination in sight, she began her run. Most of her neighborhood knew she would occasionally run at night so they would watch out for her. Holly took off in the direction of the park taking in all the fresh air. She ran past the lake and continued until she got downtown.

What in the world are you thinking woman? You are way too far from home. I need to call Brandon. Ughhh I can't though, he's on a date.

She had stopped running long enough to catch her breath and slow her breathing down. From the corner of her eye she thought she saw Brandon, just as she took off again. She did a double take and didn't see where she was running, and she ran smack dab into the door of a parked car. The owner had just opened it and was about to get out.

"Oh, my goodness ma'am is you okay?" the guy asked as he stepped out of the Infinity sedan.

Holly didn't know what to think as she managed to stand up. She was running fast enough to get knocked to the ground. The gentleman was reaching to help her up, but Holly wasn't having it.

"I'm okay but you should probably watch out for others."

"I didn't expect anyone to be running this time of night ma'am I assure you. Can I take you to the hospital? On me of course."

"No, thank you. I will be okay."

As she turned to walk away, she collapsed down onto one knee.

"Help! Help!" the guy yelled.

Holly tried to insist that she was okay. The more she tried to stand the more he kept holding her still. She heard a familiar voice hovering over her.

"Holly, what in the world?" Brandon turned his attention toward the guy. "What happened?'

"Hey, I'm Gene, she ran into my car door just as I was opening it. I think she got the wind knocked out of her. She was fine sort of and then when she turned to walk off, she went down. Man, I promise I offered to get her to a hospital, at my expense."

Gene could see the anger building up in Brandon. He continued trying to diffuse the situation. By this time, the lady that was with Brandon had also walked over to join them but was keeping her distance. Embarrassed by the fuss that was being made over her, Holly began to stand up again. This time Brandon helped her.

"Are you alright? Seriously are you alright?"

"Just a little dizzy, but I promise I'm okay. Everyone please go back to what you were doing."

Brandon looked over at his companion, she nodded her head without him saying a word. She smiled to herself because they were just speaking about this woman.

Brandon took control of the situation and says he will take it from there. Gene backed up and offered his apologizes once again. Brandon escorted Holly to his car. He helped her inside. Closing the door for her, she looked so pitiful.

Before he could speak, Holly was in tears.

"Stop that. Are you hurting anywhere? Shall we make a trip to the ER?"

Wiping her eyes and reaching in his glovebox for a piece of Kleenex, she exhaled in between the sobs.

"I just want to go home. I ran too far from the house. I did not mean to, but I was frustrated with crap on my mind. Then I saw you and I wasn't paying attention and I ran into the guy's door. I'm an idiot. I just want to go home, please."

Without a word, he put the car in reverse and pulled into the direction of taking her home. These last few weeks, it's been harder and harder to get a read on her. He thought of all the people in this world, he knew Holly without a doubt. She was proving him wrong day by day.

They arrived at her house, Brandon got out and opened her door, helping her out of the car.

"Lean into me and stop being an ass. Hand me your key please."

Holly complied she knew when to keep her mouth closed, well most of the time she did. She allowed Brandon to do what he always did, and that was take care of her for a bit. This man was truly amazing. He helped her to the bathroom so she could shower.

"I'll be out here, if you need my help to make it to the bed or do you want to go to the couch?" he said as he closed the door partially. He wanted to be able to hear her if she needed help.

"The bed is fine. Will you stay with me or do you need to go?"

"I'm here, I'm always here."

A moment later he heard the shower going, another moment later he hears Holly groaning. He felt bad for her, but he was limited on what he could do. Besides, she would never ask him to help her shower. She was too independent for that nonsense.

This was by far the hardest shower Holly ever took. Several times she wanted to call out for Brandon to help her, but she pushed through it. *Suck it up Holly. Stop being a baby. You can do this.* She gave herself a pep talk the entire time. The hot water felt good on her body. For a moment she was able to forget the pain. When she wasn't focused on the pain her mind went to Brandon. He was probably going to go off on her eventually. She inadvertently did to him what he did to her. He must think she was crazy. She ruined his date, and now he is stuck here taking care of her and her clumsy self.

She is my mess. I know this. I guess I have always known. I just need to get her to realize it.

Brandon was wracking his brain trying to understand, why was she so far from home. Did he tell her and not remember where he would be?

Brandon knew this was easier to say than do. He made his way to the kitchen to fix her some hot tea, and to get her some Aleve from the cabinet. Once he was done, he returned to her bedroom and turned the television on to one of her favorites *The Prodigal Son*. Although he had been in her bedroom too many times to count, this time felt different. He couldn't explain it, but it felt a little uneasy, like everything had changed somehow. Brandon was sitting on the edge of the bed when Holly opened the door to the bathroom. He immediately got up to assist her to the bed. She smiled and scowled in pain right after. Brandon put his hand on her stomach to steady her as she leaned into him.

"Ouch!"

"I'm sorry. Just trying to help here."

"I know and I do appreciate it."

Once they made it to the bed, she opened her robe up so that he could see the bruising on her torso. Brandon forgot to breath for a minute. Trying to stay focused on the issues at hand, he became angry looking at her that way. Inside he knew it was her fault but still something hurt her. He somehow failed her; he was supposed to always protect her. His mind began to wander even further away. *What if something worse would have happened? What if he hadn't been right there?*

"Hey. Snap out of it. Whatever you were thinking, I'm okay."

Brandon looked down at her stomach and gestured with his hand and made a facial expression that said, 'like really?'

Shaking his head, he helped her to get into bed. He put an extra pillow behind her head to make sure she would stay up to watch tv for a bit. He knew if she went to bed too soon, she would be up in the wee hours of the morning. While on her side of the bed, he fed her the Aleve and held her cup for her to sip the tea.

"You good for a bit? I'm going to run home and shower and grab my clothes for tomorrow."

"I'm okay, but you do remember you have a few outfits here right. When we got back from Jamaica, you left some clothes here. But if you just want to go home you can. You don't have to stay here. I will be okay; I just want to lay here."

"You just trying to get me to stay. Where's the clothes at?" Brandon said jokingly. "I'm going to jump in the shower really quick, try not to, I don't know kill yourself."

After surviving her glaring eyes, he grabbed his stuff out of her double closet. He noticed his things were neatly hung up to the far right. Holly was funny that way, she slept on the left side of the bed, and her clothes were to the left. She had terrible OCD and sometimes it showed more than others.

Brandon grabbed his clothing and headed to the shower. He began to disrobe and was halfway through before he realized he didn't have a towel. Starting the water before he stepped out of the bathroom shirtless and barefoot to grab a towel from the hall linen closet.

As much as Holly wanted to pretend that she didn't feel his presence even in her current state, she was very aware of him. Usually his trademark scent of Mercedes for Men, would give her reason to pause a bit. With his shirt off it permeated through the room, lingering well after he reentered the bathroom to take his shower. Holly had always thought Brandon was fine, but she always saw him as a bit of a geek also. It had always been easier to keep her mind clear to make sure he stayed within the friendship zone. Most days she started to doubt that was the best course of action.

By the time Brandon finished his shower, Holly was into a somber sleep, snoring and all. Normally Brandon hated to hear someone snore, but hers never seemed to bother him. He thought it sounded cute as far as snoring went. Brandon had dried off while in the bathroom and put on his pajama bottoms, opting to leave his shirt off. He hated sleeping with a shirt on, he always felt constricted. After making sure the door was locked and the covers were pulled up around Holly, he went around to the opposite side of the bed and got in. Almost immediately he felt Holly stir and turn towards him. Brandon had slept in her bed many times; this time was different. Turning over he tried to clear his mind and concentrate on sleep. Before too long he was out, but his mind was far from clear.

Holly awakened to find she had slid herself all the way into Brandon's arms. Her head was lying on his chest. His breathing and heartbeat had been her lullaby. Her first thoughts were, how did I get this close to him? This is not safe Holly, she kept reminding herself. Her thoughts didn't seem to stop as she began rubbing her hand up his muscular chest, he began to stir. Knowing she should stop but his stirring ignited some feelings she was unaware of until that moment.

Her leg was so close to his inner thigh that she could feel the thumping of his manhood as he began to stiffen. Holly slid her leg closer and closer until she could feel him on her leg. She moaned and inhaled at the feel of that skin to skin. Holly eased up on her side, ignoring the pain that radiated through her.

Brandon's eyes opened and he smiled sleepily.

"What are you doing? This isn't supposed to happen."

Holly brought her finger to his lips and mouthed "shhhhhhhh", and Brandon listened. Looking deep into his eyes, she leaned in to kiss him. Her lips lingered upon his, willing his lips to part as her tongue invaded the depths of his mouth. She could hear the moan from him, as he wrapped his arm around her, pulling her fully on top of him. Holly wasn't satisfied with this. At this moment she was craving him, needing to feel him inside of her. She raised up to a sitting position and she lowered herself onto him.

Holly woke up startled. Looking over to Brandon who had awakened as well.

"You okay? Are you hurting?" he asked with concern in his voice.

"'I'm okay. Go back to sleep. I promise I'm okay."

Holly had never been so embarrassed than at that present moment. *What is going on? What is happening to me? That collision must have really done a number on me.*

Laying back down and turning over onto her side, making sure she wasn't facing Brandon, she let out a sigh. After an hour of twisting and turning she finally went to sleep.

CHAPTER NINE

The next morning, Brandon was the first to wake up. He showered and got dressed and made breakfast. By the time he finished, Holly was shuffling into the kitchen.

"Hey sleepy head. How are you feeling?"

"I'm okay. Just a little tired and sore."

Brandon looked down and he could see her torso was bruised still. He asked if she wanted to go to the hospital again. Of course, she said no, as he knew she would.

"Smells good in here. I need to have you here more often." Holly joked.

The two of them had tried it years ago and it was fun. Her comment took them both down memory lane for a moment, until the smoke alarm sounded. The last of the pancakes he left on the griddle were burnt.

"Oh crap! I'm sorry." Brandon said unplugging the griddle.

"You're good. Otherwise breakfast smells great. Thank you."

They both sat down, neither one of them really saying much. Both were feeling a little awkward and that was a new feeling for them. Halfway into the meal, Brandon attempted to break the ice and ask if she was going to be okay when he left to go to work.

"I'm fine. Truly I am, and again I am sorry about ruining your date last night." smiling she added, "I guess we are even."

Brandon thought his previous mistake was forgiven, obviously she still held it against him, even if it was in a small way. He hated that he had lost a part of her trust. They finished breakfast in silence. Brandon got up to leave for work. He grabbed his jacket, then walking over to Holly, hugged her, and kissed her, and told her to call if she needed anything. And with that he was gone.

The events from the previous night, her dream and how Brandon acted this morning left her with an uneasy feeling. Shaking it off as much as she could Holly decides it is best to just focus on herself. She decided to work from home to allow herself sometime to stop hurting so bad. Looking at the time on her watch, she decided to call Cherise before it got too late in the morning. She shuffled to her bedroom to grab her cell phone. Holly dialed her secretary however she didn't answer, so she decided to send her a text and an email asking her to cancel any meetings scheduled at the office. Holly told Cherise to see if anyone wanted to do a conference call instead and if so send her the times. Cherise responded within moments of Holly pressing send. The two ladies chatted back and forth for a bit, and Holly explained that she was hurting, Cherise told her not to worry about it that she had the office covered.

Even before she said it Holly knew she could depend on

Cherise. She had never let her down since she hired her 6 years ago.

"Cherise, you are a life saver. Remind me to add a bonus to your check this month."

Cherise thanked Holly and told her again she had the office taken care of. She only needed to rest and feel better. Cherise insisted that Holly take Tuesday off as well.

"I'll check in later and let you know if I feel any better or if I need you to reschedule." she paused and then added "On second thought, I will take tomorrow too. Thank you. Call me or email me if you come across any problems."

Grabbing her laptop, she climbed back onto the bed. *The bed she shared with Brandon*, she thought as she looked at the place where he laid a few short hours ago. Her thoughts began to trail off.

Brandon occupied her thoughts, but he was not alone. She began to wonder about how this date with Alexander was going to go. Thoughts of Trey even popped into her head.

She opened her email and began to work, only to find her mind kept wandering. Her stomach was also hurting as she was in a sitting position on the bed. To get some relief she closed the laptop and grabbed her phone and laid on her back. She began to respond to emails through her phone. This took a bit longer than she would have liked but at least her midsection wasn't hurting as bad.

Holly was on her last email reply when her phone dings. She ignores it, but within minutes it sounded off again. For the second time she ignored the message that was coming through. After she finished with her email she clicked on the message. It was from Trey.

"Hey gorgeous. I was just messaging you to catch up. It has been a few days. Hope everything is well."

Holly told him that all was okay. She started to tell him about her accident but for some reason, she didn't feel he needed to be concerned with that.

"I enjoyed our outing the other day. I was hoping for another, do you think that is possible?"

Holly started to type but then erased it five times. She was second guessing her response. Trey must have sensed something because he started typing.

"Is everything okay? I thought we had a good time?"

"I did. We did. I just have some things going on right now that I need to get sorted out."

"Oh." was Trey's only response

"It's not you. It is just bad timing."

Holly felt ashamed for using that line because it was so cliché. She didn't know what else to tell him. She couldn't very well tell him she felt nothing when they kissed.

"Well so much for bad timing. I guess I will let you do what you need to do. If you change your mind, I'll be around, maybe." he added as an afterthought.

That made Holly smile to herself. *Oh, he is being cocky. Guess I made the right decision. Thank you for that.* She thought about immediately blocking him on the site, but she opted not to, it wasn't that serious.

The next day was more of the same, hurting, laying around, and trying to stay on top of her emails. That night she started to feel a little better although the bruise on her torso had turned dark, it was less painful. She was assuredly going to work at the office tomorrow. Holly never liked being stuck in the house and the last two days of solitude drove her crazy.

She texted Brandon just to say hey. It was weird that he hadn't checked on her all day. *Get over it.* She kept telling herself. When he replied it was cordial but not the usual. He kept saying that he was just busy with work and that everything else was good. He even apologized for them not doing their weekly lunch date. Holly wasn't in any condition anyway to partake.

Holly finally managed to get up and about on Thursday and headed to the office. Cherise had done a great job of holding things together for her. When she arrived on Thursday, she had her day planned out and the schedule on her desk as usual. She was even thoughtful enough to only schedule two meetings for the afternoon.

Midway through the day her phone goes off and it is a message from Alexander.

"I was just checking in on you. Messaged you yesterday or so I thought. Message was stuck in the drafts box."

"Hey. Thanks for checking on me. It seems as if it has been a bit since we chatted."

" You're not thinking about backing out on Friday, are you?" Alexander inquired.

Holly hesitated and let out a deep sigh before she replied to him.

"To be honest I was. Earlier this week I hurt myself and I didn't know if I was going to feel better by then. Today is my first day back at work. Thank God, I'm the boss." She laughed.

"If we need to plan for another time, it's cool. My apologizes for not checking in on you sooner. I've had a few things come up at work and with my family."

"I'm feeling better so we can keep the date. Besides, I'm ready to see if Madame Croix is worth all the rave reviews, she has been getting since she opened."

They chatted more for a while, until it was time for the last of her meetings.

"I got to go. I have a meeting to get ready for. See you tomorrow at 7:30 sharp."

"Yes, see you then."

Holly decided to reach out to Brandon to see if he responds, his phone goes to voicemail. She leaves him a quick message to say she was going out tomorrow and she would check back with him to see if he wanted to hang out on Sunday. Holly also wanted to get his opinion on if going on this date was going to be a good idea or not. she was beginning to realize that more and more Brandon had brushed her off. Holly had gotten used to depending on him, she began to see she was going to have to start taking care of herself and making the important decisions by herself. For once, she was going to have to take charge. Something she hadn't done on her own in years.

As an afterthought Holly remembered she needed to get something to wear for dinner tomorrow. Of course, it was just another reason to go shopping. By the time she made it home it was almost 10. She was exhausted and her midsection started to hurt a little.

Making her way to get some medicine from the cabinet in the kitchen before she started the shower. Moments later she was in the shower, enjoying the feeling of the hot water thrumming against her skin. It even felt good against her stomach. For a moment she was relaxed, so much so that her mind drifted off, landing smack dab on Brandon. She envisioned what he must have looked like while in that same shower just days before. She wondered what would have happened if she had walked in and started showering with him.

Snap out of it. What is really going on with me?

Holly had never had these thoughts before until recently, at least none that she remembered. She kept telling herself to get it together. She finished up her shower and headed to bed. Before long she was sleeping soundly.

Friday finally arrived and she was starting to get a little excited about the dinner plans for later. First, she must make it through a few meetings and a quick hair appointment. The day went off without a hitch that is until she got to the hair salon. Ebony wasn't going to be denied any information. She wanted to know all she could about these dates Holly had been on. Holly indulged her and told her about the terrific time she had on the picnic. She even explained how tonight's dinner was just a meal between friends.

"Uh-huh. You expect me to believe that? What is going on with your boy? He is just so cute to me."

Holly shook her head and sighed.

"He is doing his own thing these days. I think he has found someone, and they have been dating. We don't talk about that part much right now."

Ebony had a stunned look on her face. Those two have always been thick as thieves. They shared everything. Something wasn't right.

"Girl if you don't stop overthinking stuff and let's get this hair done so I can get home, shower and change my clothes. I would like to be fresh and clean before dinner tonight."

"Like I said, uh-huh. If it was just a friendly meal you wouldn't be tripping." she said as she laughed.

It was useless to argue with her. Holly knew it was just a meal between friends. She had nothing to prove. How dare Ebony try and play her, she knows she like to stay cute.

Holly had told Brandon about Ebony's obsession over him. He didn't entertain it at all. Since then he tried to avoid going to the shop, he didn't want to give her false hope.

As if reading her mind, as she was walking out the door all she could hear was Ebony giggling.

"Tell that cutie to come on through. It's been a long time since he stopped by. We got some lost time to make up for."

Holly didn't even respond as she bolted through the door. She loved Ebony's work, but sometimes that mouth. She was good for a great laugh though at times. *So, I guess it all balances out.*

By the time Holly reached home, it was 5:30, no time for a quick nap. She put her work bag away.

"Alexa play my playlist, It's a Vibe."

Her playlist began to play as she grabbed her new body wash to match her Mercedes perfume. That was her favorite, and Brandon's as well. For Valentine's Day last year, they bought each other a gift set of it. Why did her thoughts keep going back to Brandon?

After showering and getting dressed, she sent a text to Brandon. Out of habit she still wanted him to know where she was just in case something happened. He shot back a quick, *"I got it"*. *At least he responded,* she thought. That was better than nothing.

At 7 o'clock she was leaving the house. The restaurant was twenty minutes away, and usually traffic wasn't bad. She made it there without speeding too bad, in just fifteen minutes. She decided to wait a few before going inside, she didn't want to appear too overeager.

Already inside her date was waiting, becoming more and more anxious by the minute. He made sure he was seated so he could face the door and see her when she came in. He thought about turning his back to her, but then he didn't want to have to guess when she arrived. Truthfully, he wanted to see her face when she came in. He was nervous and that wasn't his usual thing.

Holly walked through the door and the maître d was waiting. She told him she was meeting a friend name Alexander. The maître d smiled and told her to follow him. As she did, they rounded a corner and there was Brandon. Holly waved at him as he smiled at her. Several thoughts flashed through her mind in what seemed like eternity, but reality was on a few short seconds. *He must be here with his date too,* Holly thought. Unless he was here to sabotage this date as well, but he couldn't be.

Brandon stands up as the maître d guided Holly closer to his table.

"She is with me."

Holly's face had a bewildered look. She turned to her guide and told him this was must be a mistake. Brandon intervened.

CHAPTER TEN

"*H*olly, I need to explain. Will you please sit?"

"Brandon, what's going on? Where is Alexander? Please don't tell me you acted a fool before I got here?"

"Holly, please sit down. Do not cause a scene. I promise to explain it all to you."

Brandon was a little hurt that she thought he would violate her trust again. He had promised that he wouldn't. Did that not mean anything?

Before Brandon could begin the waiter brought them some champagne and some soup. Brandon had preordered for her. After he filled their glasses, they both sipped and agreed it was good. He left the bottle on the table for them. Once he walked away, Brandon was the first to speak.

"I know you had a date tonight."

"Brandon, I don't understand?"

"It's simple Holly, I'm Alexander. You know the guy with no profile picture. Before you get started, I need you to hear me out, please."

Seeing the look of hurt in her eyes, almost brought him to

tears. Not that he was a soft man, but for her he was and always would be.

"We've known each other for what seems like a lifetime to me, but you didn't even remember my middle name. It stings, but it afforded me this opportunity to get to know you on a different level. I thought I knew everything about you. I was wrong. You are so much more than I thought."

Brandon took a dramatic pause, to gather his thoughts and to see if she was going to jump in, she didn't, and so he continued.

"None of this was meant to be deceptive. To be honest I thought you would have caught on when I didn't have a photo. As Alexander I could be supportive of your dating, whereas me, it was tearing me apart inside. The crazy part is that all these emotions that I am now feeling happened out of nowhere. One moment we were just cool, then you wanted to date."

The waiter cleared his throat as he interrupted their conversation to place their meals on the table. He asked if they needed anything to which they both shook their heads no. Within seconds he was gone. Holly began immediately.

"Are you kidding me? You purposely didn't tell me who you were. Why, what's with all the secrets?"

"I don't have an answer for you. I guess I was a little scared and this is new to me. The night I slept over because you threw yourself into that dude's car door, something in me stirred. When you and Trey were at dinner, that got under my skin. I know it is hypocritical of me."

"You're damn right it is. You have been dating this one and that one. Never once did you say anything to me about feelings, but you pop up in my inbox on an app you designed no less. Ughhhhh."

Holly was annoyed at herself just as much as with him.

She allowed him to voice his feelings while she stayed silent. Did she dare tell him she had dreamt of him. She would have to if she were to be honest.

"Brandon, I have been spoiled by you for so long I think I took it for granted that you would always be there when I needed you. I forgot to show you that I appreciate you and everything you do. Apparently somewhere, somehow, I fell in love with you. I'm not even sure when it started but I know it is real. I denied it for as long as I could, but that night I was running. I didn't know you were there, but you were, that was a sign. I will admit that night when we slept together, I dreamt of you. I dreamt of you holding me."

"That wasn't a dream. Somehow you ended up in my arms and I didn't move, until I got up the next morning. You were so comfortable and peaceful I couldn't disturb you. Wait, did you just say you love me?"

Holly nodded as a grin crept over her face. He really was the smartest slowest person sometimes.

"I've known it deep down that you were it for me, I just didn't want to risk what we have. I couldn't take that."

Brandon reached over to grab Holly's hand; he began rubbing the back of her fingers as he was talking.

"Holly, I know this started off wrong, but will you go out with me, Brandon Alexander Thompson?"

"I guess so. My other prospects are out the window at this point." Holly attempted a joke.

Both appearing satisfied with the outcome of the conversation, sat back and relaxed and enjoyed their dinner. It was their first as an official couple. They talked like they had never talked before and it felt good. It felt natural to them.

"Are you coming over after dinner? I mean this is usually the time, something happens, and I need your help anyway." Again, she tried to make a funny. Brandon just laughed.

"That is something you don't have to worry about again."

"Wait a minute, who was that woman the other night?

"That was my cousin Sophia, she was having some guy trouble. Remember she is the one from Boston, you spoke with her on the phone a couple of times."

Holly did in fact remember that he had mentioned she would be coming into town. She needed a breather from Luca, her stalker of an ex-boyfriend. He had begun making trouble at her job and being an attorney who was working on becoming a partner, it did not sit well with the good ole boys at the firm. Before it got out of hand, she decided to take a leave of absence to get it sorted.

They finished their meal and Brandon walks around to her chair and pulls it back for to stand. When she does, he pulls her close enough so she can feel his breath on her face. No matter when it was, his breath was always fresh. How did he do it, even after eating was beyond her, but she was not going to complain. Brandon looked her in the eyes as he placed his hand on her chin and tilted her mouth up to him.

"I love you." were the simple words he uttered as he took her mouth with his. Shivers shot through Holly as they kissed, it was not the sparks she heard of, but the shivers she felt were even better. It was her that spoke up first.

"Let's go home."

They walked out of the restaurant hand in hand for the first time, but not the last.

EPILOGUE

The first year of Holly and Brandon's new relationship had been glorious. There were a few ups and downs with getting used to each other in this new capacity. Brandon moved in with Holly after 3 months. Now that the two finally figured it out they didn't want to waste any unnecessary time. Holly was happier than ever, and she finally was able to tell Ebony that Brandon was off limits. Brandon popped the question on their six-month anniversary, and they were going to be married in another six months. Life was good. Holly had another secret that would not keep much longer; she was going to give Brandon a son. The thing was none of this was planned but it all felt so right. Holly had spent most of her time planning out how she wanted her life, when what she needed was there in front of her all the while. She was given a chance to have her very own love. Holly was finally happy.

Thank You for Reading!

Don't forget to sign up for
Mind Flow Publishing & Production LLC's Newsletter @
www.mindflowpublishingproduction.com

Email us for autographed or additional paperback copies @
mindflowpubpro@gmail.com

Other Titles Also Available Include

Mental Interlude—Poetry
The Mary B Chronicles 1- 4—Fiction
Journey to Living (Kindle Only)—Inspirational
Simple Complexity—Poetry
Spoken From The Heart—Poetry
Dreams Do Come True (Kindle Only)—Fiction
Charisma's Homecoming—Fiction
For Her Love—Fiction
Falling In Love With Poetry—Poetry

Available Through:
Amazon
Barnes & Noble
Kindle

COMING SOON

Freedom In The Cage Series—Fiction
Flint
Steel
Brick
Stone
Royalty—Romantic Comedy
To Be Chosen—Paranormal
Finding Kate—Suspense Thriller

Upcoming Titles Will Be Available Through:
Amazon
Barnes & Noble
Kindle
Apple iBooks
Kobo

ABOUT THE AUTHOR

Although I'm still considered new to the publishing world, I have hit the ground running full speed ahead. In my first year, I was signed to Mind Flow Publishing & Production LLC, and I have published a total of 6 books. I have earned Amazon's Best Sellers Top 100 orange banner. My works are spread across several genres such as; Poetry, Inspirational, Urban Fiction and Christian Fiction. I will be trying my hand at cozy mysteries, romance, and suspense thrillers. My love for writing started when I was about twelve, writing poetry and writing speeches for various oratorical contests. Inspiration for my craft is pulled from my own life experiences, as well as others. I have been featured on several podcasts, as well as Up and Coming Authors Newsletters. When I'm not writing, I love to design shadowboxes, and create personalized greeting cards. I have released my 3rd poetry book (Spoken from the Heart) in August 2019. Some of my current books available are The Mary B Chronicles 1 - 4, Mental Interlude, and Journey to Living, Simple Complexity, Dreams Do Come True, Spoken from the Heart, For Her Love and Charisma's Homecoming. All of which are available on Amazon, and www.mindflowpublishingproduction.com.

Made in the USA
Monee, IL
21 July 2020